THE ARRANGEMENT 17
THE FERRO FAMILY

By:

H.M. WARD

www.SexyAwesomeBooks.com

COPYRIGHT

H.M. WARD PRESS
First Edition: November 2014
ISBN: 9781630350482

THE ARRANGEMENT 17

Dear Reader,

The Arrangement Series is different. How? The story is organic—and growing swiftly. Originally intended to be four serial novels, fans of the series demanded more Sean & Avery, spurring an entirely new concept: a fan-driven series. When fans ask for more, I write more.

I am astonished and humbled by the response this series has received. As the series grows, I am constantly fascinated by the requests and insights from readers. This series has sold over 4 MILLION copies! The average length of each book is 125 pages in paperback and can be read in a few hours or less.

This series intertwines with my other work, but is designed to be read independently, as a quick read between other titles. You can join in the discussion via my Facebook page: www.facebook.com/AuthorHMWard. For a complete listing of Ferro books, look here: www.SexyAwesomeBooks.com & click BOOKS.

Thank you and happy reading!

~Holly

Chapter 1

Hearts pounding, Peter and I drive through the grounds of the formerly world famous Oak Beach Inn. Once upon a time, the elite of New York City would gather here each weekend and party until sunrise in the old mansion built right on the waterfront. It was a great spot back in the day, but over time it suffered enough neglect that it finally closed—despite the best efforts of historic preservationists. No matter how hard they tried, they couldn't save the

OBI. Shortly after closing, most of the mansion burned in a fire. Add in a hurricane that ate half the coastline, and now it has the solemn feel of a graveyard. No one dances here anymore. There's no laughter or smiles, just cold damp fear.

Peter's body tenses in the driver's seat. His hand moves to open his door and get out with me, but I reach over him and put my hand over his. Gently, I move his hand off of the door handle and back to the steering wheel.

"You're not supposed to be here," I say firmly. "I have no idea what he'll do to me or to Sean if you linger. Go."

"Avery, this guy is unstable. He could kill you."

"He won't." Peter looks at me like I'm mental, but it's a feeling I've had deep in my gut since I saw Marty shoot Sean. The blaring music and the flashing lights nearly blinded me on stage, but I know I saw him there. "Peter, please trust me. Marty had so many chances to hurt me already. He would have killed me by now if that was his plan."

Peter grips the wheel hard enough to make his knuckles turn white and stares at his fingers. Inhaling deeply, he shifts his blue gaze to the side, his eyes searching mine. "I do trust you. It's him I don't trust—he's off. There's something about him that doesn't sit right with me. Add in the shit with Sean, and I think you going in there is a bad move." His eyes are soulful as he speaks, as if he's pleading with me to reconsider.

He's right, of course, but there isn't another way. "Peter, the thing is, my life is so messed up right now I can't go anywhere without someone threatening to hurt me. I know you mean well, but I have to do this. I'll get Sean back."

Peter looks as if he wants to argue, but begrudgingly stays seated. He mashes his lips together, swallows some words he decides not to say, and sighs deeply. His shoulders slump a little and I know he won't fight me anymore. I'm not entirely sure how he talked me into letting him drive me out here in the first place. He's sneaky like his brother, but he cares about me and he cares about Sean—that much I know.

Peter runs his hands through his hair and glances over at me from behind the steering wheel. "Mel will come for you if you're not back in this spot in an hour. That woman scares the hell out of me. I'm sure she'll kill Marty if he hurts you, and she'll have fun doing it. By the way, why are all your closest friends mental?"

Mel is a handful and has had a hard life. She knows how to take care of herself, but I don't think she's killed anyone. People still think she's responsible for the dead hooker in Sean's hotel room, but I know it wasn't her. Once she knows a person, and likes them, Mel drops her guard. The sad part is there are very few people she can relax around, so they only know the version of Mel that's a little rough around the edges.

I bump Peter with my shoulder and wave my finger at him while speaking, trying not to smile. "Come on Mr. Poet, you already know the answer to that. Friends are a reflection of oneself. You might want to reconsider that thing you've got going on with Mr. Turkey."

Peter laughs. "Better go over to the tall dark grass now before the crazy guy comes looking for you." I squeeze his hand and hop out of his sleek black car, slamming the door behind me. Peter puts down the passenger window and leans across the seat. "Be careful." His eyes are locked on mine, and we both jump, startled, when a voice comes from the shadows behind me.

"Oh, she will be." Marty steps out from the shadows and lunges at me. He completely ignores Peter, who is swearing and kicking his door open, ready to follow us.In an instant, I feel myself being carried away from the car and into the darkness. His hand is over my mouth, stifling my scream.

Chapter 2

I bite down on the flesh of Marty's palm and he releases me, spewing curses while he does it. Stomping my foot down hard, I crush his toes. He's wearing velvet lounge slippers, and wails like a baby. I don't have time to wonder why he's dressed for bed—Marty always dresses weird. When we first met, I thought it was because he was gay. The asshole used my assumption to get close to me. Repressed anger rears its head from deep within me.

Marty shot Sean.

Growling wildly, I round on him, ready to fight. I want my fists in his face. I want to hear his nose crunch and cause him as much pain as he caused Sean.

Just before my knee lifts to hit him in the tenders, he grabs my shoulders and leans in. "Stop."

It's one word, one request that changes everything. If I wander off with him, things could get worse. I pause for a second, waiting for him to say something else or fight back, but he doesn't.

Peter remains by his car, silently watching, his eyes narrowed into slits. His body is poised and prepared, ready to run over and save me. I can't let him do that. I have to find out where Marty took Sean and this is the only way. I shake my head at Peter, warning him to stay there. He flinches and grits his teeth, but he doesn't move any further toward us.

Lifting my hand in a gesture of peace, I nod at Marty. "Take me to Sean."

Marty shakes his head and looks from me to Peter's car. "You know, I can't fucking believe this, Avery. I told you to come alone. You deliberately disobeyed my request and came with not just anyone, but one of the Ferro brothers. Then you break my foot instead of saying hello." He mutters to himself for a moment, and then glances at the car, agitated. "Tell Ferro to take a hike or you won't like how this goes."

Marty's hair is a mess and he's wearing rich guy pajamas. He reminds me of a young Hugh Hefner, wearing a velvet robe and tasseled belt. How has no one noticed him, dressed like that? The police must be blind not to notice this guy. He's on the beach, in velvet slippers, with no car. Where's a state trooper when you need one? I glance up and down the road, but it's empty.

Heart hammering, I ask, "Where are we going?"

"Stop asking questions and do as I say, or you'll never see Sean again." He hooks an arm around my waist and glares at Peter. "Your choice, Avery. We can do this the easy way or the hard way."

My entire body is shaking. It's beyond a minor tremble and I hate it for betraying me. Marty laughs lightly, shaking his head. "You finally figured out you should be afraid of me? It fucking took long enough."

Marty yanks his arm, pulling my back to his front. I feel something hard and round pressed against my spine. He shouts to Peter, "Get out of here, unless you want me to put a bullet in her back. I'm guessing the Ferro clan doesn't want another dead woman on their hands."

Peter yells back, "No one would think I killed her."

"I wouldn't be too sure. Once a Ferro, always a Ferro, isn't that right Pete?" The use of his old name makes Peter's shoulders stiffen and I wonder what secrets he's hiding. The principal with the turkey vulture and the sweet girlfriend is the Peter I know, but Marty knows something more—something dark.

Peter turns his eyes toward me. "One hour. That's it. Then Mel comes for you—fuck that, I'll come for you—and I guarantee you won't like it." Peter's voice is low and lethal. For the first time, I see a strong resemblance to Sean. The look he gives Marty promises pain.

"Drive away, Pete. She'll be right here an hour from now." Marty holds me tight, pinning me against the barrel of his gun.

"Go, it's all right." I mean to sound confident, but my voice is shaking.

Peter swears, jumps back in his car, and peels out, leaving me alone with Marty. I watch his taillights shrink to nothing as his black car is swallowed by the night.

Chapter 3

Marty inhales deeply and removes the gun from my back. There are too many emotions going through me at the moment to nail one down, so they all come flying out. The second the gun is down, I round on him and knee his nuts. Marty yelps and bends forward. My knee comes up again and connects with his nose. Meanwhile my hands ball into fists, hitting him every chance I get. I'm screaming at him, bellowing, "How could you?"

His betrayal snakes around my throat and tightens until I can't stand it. I lash out at him with renewed energy, hitting him over and over.

Marty shrieks, "Holy fuck, Avery! Cut it out! Stop or I'll make you stop."

Rage takes over my body and my brain struggles to keep up. My body continues to tremble, but not from fear. "Bullshit! That's what this is! That's what you are! You don't even have him, do you? This was just another invention to get me naked or some other stupid shit. I hate you! I hate you, Marty!"

I grab both sides of his head by his ears and tug, hard. Shocked, his face comes flying toward mine and I head-butt him. We collide with a loud *thunk*. Marty swears, nearly falling over. Since I'm not a ninja, the momentum knocks me on my ass, my head throbbing in pain. I touch my forehead and feel warm blood on my fingers. Rage flashes across my face—I can't hide it. I jump and lunge at him, screaming while I do so.

"I trusted you, you bastard!"

"Fine, the hard way it is." Marty reaches for me as I rush at him. He catches me by the shoulders and the momentum of being jerked to a stop makes my feet go flying. I land on my back and let out an *oof* sound. I barely have time to catch my breath before Marty covers my face with a white cloth. I try not to breathe, but I can't hold my breath. When I finally suck in air, it tastes too sweet and burns my throat. Marty pins me to the ground, as I claw at his hands, trying to get the cloth off my face. It's poisoned. No, it's not—oh no. My head feels light and I start blinking. My body goes limp and before I can figure out why, I lose control of my hands and they flop to the pavement. I stare up at the inky sky with its spattering of stars, watching Marty remove the cloth.

As he pulls it away and my eyes flutter shut, I notice two letters on the handkerchief.

S. F.

The world fades to black.

Chapter 4

My head is screaming when I start to regain consciousness. It feels like it's made of lead and possibly in a vice. It seems a great deal fatter than normal, or maybe it just feels that way. I try to open my eyes but they're too heavy. I try again, but still no results. Sound begins to penetrate the fog surrounding me. I lie still and listen to two voices arguing heatedly in hushed tones.

"...then we wouldn't be in this situation!"

"If you hadn't interfered, none of this would have happened, Ferro. This is your fault. You think I wanted to do this to her? She's insane when she's mad. You know that."

"I told you to do it first thing, not to wait and talk to her. You jeopardized the whole operation, and risked Pete finding out. You're a sorry excuse for a—"

My eyes flutter open involuntarily and Marty talks over him, "Shut it, dipshit. She's awake and as soon as that headache passes, she's going to bolt. Stop wasting time and start talking." Marty is watching me with a softened expression on his face, which confuses the crap out of me. Hell, this whole scene confuses the crap out of me.

I blink and try to push up. Sean rushes to my side and puts a hand on my shoulder, stopping me. As his fingers clutch my shoulders, his voice softens a little. "It's too soon. Wait or you'll be sick."

"You're here." I smile at him. He's safe. "You're all right." Marty didn't hurt him. In fact, he seems better than the last time I saw him. He was hurt, recovering from a bullet wound. Leaning over me like that should make him hurt. Sean should be groaning from pain, but he's not.

Something is off. Even sedated, I can feel it. I sense it, but I still can't figure out what's going on. Add in what I just heard and my eyes widen. Sean Ferro, the initials.

My heart twists. "Marty had your handkerchief, didn't he?"

The two letters come back into focus in my mind, the ramifications quickly follow, snapping into place. If the handkerchief was Sean's, then based on what I just heard, Sean and Marty are… I shiver. "Oh, my God, Sean! You told Marty to drug me, didn't you? I heard you say it—he was supposed to drug me. Marty tried to talk me into following him first."

Sean's emotional mask juts up and snaps firmly in place. He shows no remorse, no affection. It's like he hasn't changed at all and there's a man I don't know standing in front of me. "I did what I had to do. It was for your own good. If you were found with Marty—able to get away, but not trying—it would look wrong. They'd think you were helping him."

Outraged, I yell, "Helping him do what, exactly? Shoot you? Kidnap you? Bury you in a freakin' sand dune?" I scream the last part and wish I hadn't. My head throbs so badly, it feels like there's a steel bar vibrating in my brain. I grab my head and shut my eyes.

Clutching my temples, I growl, "Where are we?"

Sean sits by my side as Marty paces behind me. We're in an old house and I can hear the water lapping against the shore, which means we are very close to the ocean. The house is dark, save the glow of a dim light they've put in the fireplace.

"Oak Island. This house is owned by, well it's, uh—" Sean looks up at Marty. Still lying on my back, I look up at him expectantly.

"I own it." Marty moves across the dark room and sits across from me on an old velvet chair that's seen better days. He rests his elbows on his knees, leans forward, and clasps his hands together. His mop of hair falls over his eyes, hiding the cut I gave him earlier. He glares at the tattered Persian rug on the floor and growls, "Just say it Sean, or I will."

But Sean doesn't speak and neither does Marty. For a moment, the only sound I can hear is the roar of the ocean. Rain begins to bounce eerily off the dark windowpanes.

I don't know what's going on, but I feel it—things aren't right. Something is off. Annoyed with both of them, I snap, "What's going on? Contrary to popular belief, it doesn't seem like you're being held hostage, Sean."

Sean slips off the couch and kneels in front of me, taking both of my hands. "You're safe. That's all that matters." His dark hair is a tousled mess, like he's been riding his motorcycle without his helmet. There's a cut on his cheek, and three-day-old scruff on his face. Dark circles line his eyes, as if he hasn't slept since he last shaved.

"To you, maybe." Head still swimming, I'm too woozy to yell. As the room wobbles, I remember Sean is the one who did this to me. Maybe it wasn't his hand, but it was his idea. That means Sean and Marty are in this together, although I can't see how. "This makes no sense! Why is Marty here? He tried to kill you and now you're just hanging out together in a beach house?" I'm yelling again and trying to sit up.

"Lie down, Avery, or I'll tie you down instead." Sean has a wicked gleam in his eyes. I'm sure he's not kidding and I'm also sure he'd like the opportunity.

"Sean," Marty taps his watch, "time. The hour is almost up."

Sean rises and grabs his hair, tugging it in frustration. He runs his palms down the back of his neck and makes an aggravated sound in the back of his throat. Finally, he turns to look at me. "It was fake. The whole thing."

"You're not hurt?" He shakes his head. "But I saw you get shot—I saw the blood. I saw Marty with the gun."

"It was staged, Avery."

"What? How? I saw Marty holding the gun and I saw your blood. I thought you were going to die, Sean. You were barely breathing. Are you saying that was all an act? Are you saying I saw an exploding ketchup bottle?" I glance at Marty and back at Sean. "I know what I saw."

Sean's voice is soft and patient. "No, you don't. No one knows what they saw that night. It was a concert, Avery. There was smoke and flashing lights forcing your eyes to refocus every second. Marty held up his gun so they'd see him clearly raise his weapon. The rest was theatrics and luck. The strobe lights tricked your eyes into seeing something that didn't actually happen. The fog machine covered me after I fell, the dye packs were top of the line, and the people in the ambulance and at the hospital were paid off. Avery, it was all fake."

Chapter 5

My jaw is hanging open. "Why? Why would you fake being shot?" I can't believe this.

"Marty's boss put a hit on me. I did something that pissed him off and the hit was his version of payback. We orchestrated the shooting and tipped off the press to create media frenzy in the aftermath, making them think Marty took the shot. Avery, we did it all to make sure you didn't end up in the ground next to your parents."

My body goes cold as the remaining tension slips from my face. Shock makes my jaw drop. "My parents?" I think back to my mom's note and fear pierces my heart. What does he know? "What's going on? Gabe keeps warning me to run. If you don't want me to take his advice, if you want to see my face tomorrow, you better tell me—"

Marty cuts me off, "Or what, Avery? You'll run away? You'll punch me in the nuts again? Thanks for that, by the way." Marty squirms in his chair. The room is too dark to see him clearly.

Anger surges from within me. I turn to Sean. "You promised me no more lies. We were supposed to tell each other the truth, and this is what you do?"

"I know." His voice is level, stoic.

"You promised me! You said you'd tell me everything, and here's your chance. What about my parents? Tell me why the hell Marty is here with you. What the hell is going on, Sean?" My heart is thumping in my chest, threatening to explode against my ribs. My stomach sours and regret fills my mouth. "You said you were through lying to me, Sean."

My rage turns on my friend, "And Marty—what the fuck? You let me think you tried to shoot the man I love? You let me think you stabbed me in the back? How could you? Both of you! How could you?" The two of them have been using me, tossing me around like a rag doll, as if their actions won't affect me in the slightest. My anger fades. This is so Sean, so classically Sean Ferro. I gave him my heart and he's still hiding from me.

What is he so afraid of? What's behind those dark eyes that he can't let me see?

"Because I—" Marty cuts off what he was going to say and jumps to his feet. His hands fly through the air frantically, as he searches for the words to explain. "It wasn't supposed to be this way. I was supposed to get close to you, get what I needed, and then get the fuck out. Instead, I met you and I liked you." He glances at Sean like he couldn't care less what the man thinks. "Avery, I want to

~23~

protect you from all of this, but you're right in the middle of it and that's the worst place to be. I won't let them hurt you. Not now, not ever. Please believe me. I'd tell you the truth, all of it, if I could, but I can't."

Glaring at him, I don't know what to say. His words swirl in my mind like a gust of wind. I can't hold onto them without wanting to cry. He sounds sincere, but I've been jerked around too many times to believe him anymore.

"Who are you? You're not a college kid with no money if you own this house—it's worth over a million bucks, easy. And if you're working for someone who puts hits on people, you're what? An enforcer? A mercenary? Do you take orders and kill people?" I push up on my elbows and lean against the back of the chaise, finally able to at least sit up. I already knew Sean was into some messed up shit, but Marty's involvement blindsides me. "Who are you?"

Worry is pinching his face. I hear it in his voice as it tightens and gets higher. "I'm the same guy you met on campus.

I'm the same guy who held you while you slept. Avery, you know me."

Sean glances at me, shocked. "You slept with him?"

"Are you serious?" I blink at Sean. "With everything that's going on, that's what you think is messed up here?" Sean doesn't answer. Instead, he looks away.

In two steps, Marty crosses the room and shoves Sean aside, trying to take my hand.

I push further back into the chaise and away from him. "Don't touch me. Either of you." Fear taints my voice and tightens my chest. Every muscle in my body is strung tight, ready to snap.

Marty's golden eyes look away as he gives up and steps back. "Avery, I'd never hurt you. You just beat the shit out of me and I didn't even fight back."

Fear gives way to anger. It drips down my spine in a wave of hot pain. Working my jaw, I finally manage to spit out the words. "I trusted you! I trusted both of you and told you everything. You," I say to Sean, "only tell lies, and Marty—you're just as bad."

"You don't understand." Marty says, looking horrified. He glances at Sean, silently pleading for help. "I can't say no. I can't tell them I won't do it. It's not an option and now I'm in this so deep I'll be lucky if I come out alive. Thanks to Sean, I might—we might all survive."

Marty steps toward me again, careful not to touch me. He kneels and places his hand on the arm of the couch. Eye to eye, he says, "Avery, they've been aiming for *you*. The hotel room, the pilot, the other dead hookers—every murder was an attempt on you. They think you know something, and they won't stop until they either get what they want or you're out of the way."

"What are you talking about?" At first I have no clue, but then I realize what this is about. Somewhere in the back of my mind I've finally connected the dots and, consequently, terror turns my stomach into knots. "Who wants me dead?"

Sean finally speaks. "Victor Campone."

Chapter 6

"What?" My voice squeaks. That name brings a fresh dose of fear, dousing me.

Sean explains, "Your mother got into some serious shit with his men when she was younger. Your father protected her as long as he could. The night they died, you were supposed to be in that car with them. They found your family and once they had you in their sights, decided their most effective course of action was to eliminate you all. But you stayed home that night and they didn't know. Someone told them there were three people in the car. Someone lied straight to Campone's face for you. That same someone also pretended to be gay to get near you."

Shocked, I gape at Marty, unable to speak. Marty looks away, holding his hands behind his back. Campone is a drug lord and into shit so dark it makes night look like day. My stomach feels like it's suspended in a free-fall.

I glance at Sean. "And what about you?"

"What about me?" Sean stands rigid next to Marty, who has resumed his frantic pacing. Marty stops and watches Sean. They're both on edge, tense and ready to fight.

I laugh coldly and shake my head. I'm so stupid. Never in a million years did I think that someone killed my parents. They weren't murdered, they were in a car crash. It was one of those freak things that happens without purpose. I should have been in the car that night, but I had bitched to Mom that I didn't want to go. I'm supposed to be in the ground with them.

Swallowing hard, I find my words and say to Sean, "It wasn't a coincidence that you stumbled upon me that day when my car got jacked? It wasn't by chance that you were at the diner? It wasn't just happy luck that you were my first client at Miss Black's either, was it?" That's what Gabe has been trying to tell me all along, but I couldn't see it. That's why he hates Sean—he knows all this and probably more. I spit out my suspicion before I lose my nerve. "You were using me to find out whatever Campone wanted? You were just trying to get the information first, weren't you?"

"Perhaps." Sean stares at me with those intense blue eyes and his lips pressed into a hard, thin line.

I wish he'd say something. I wish he'd wrap his arms around me and tell me this is all a horrible joke, because I can't accept what it really means. Lip trembling, I force out the question. "So Marty cares about me, and you don't?

You were using me to get what you wanted. Say it, Sean. I know it's true. You used everything I told you against me." In that instant, I think of the hospital. Of everything I told him, everything we did. "You even pretended to be in pain at the hospital when I kissed you. It was all fake, all of it."

I swing my legs off the chaise and start scanning the room for exits. I can't stay here another second, but the room tips sideways again. Inhaling slowly, trying to regain control of my body, I look up at Sean. "What does a mobster want with me?"

Sean just stares at me, his lips pressed together firmly. His hands are in his pockets, and he's wearing his old leather jacket. His helmet is on a table behind him. Every last bit of this was planned, and I missed it. All our nights together, all the things I said—to both of them. Confidence dies in my mouth and I want to run, to hide, but I can't. Clutching the edge of the cushions in my hands, I squeeze hard, waiting for his response.

Instead, Marty answers, "Documents. Your mother unknowingly worked as a bookkeeper for Campone before you were born. At first, they probably looked like nothing to her, ledgers, supply lists, contracts, just regular business paperwork—but once she realized what she had, she knew Campone would be willing to kill to get it back. By then, it was too late to turn back. She was smart. Realizing the danger she was in, she ran but continued to hand in her work on time, passing it through a chain of people, as she put more and more space between herself and Victor Campone. It was weeks before Campone realized what had happened, what she knew. Campone searched for her, tracking down each person she'd come in contact with, each claiming truthfully they didn't know where she was or what she knew. He didn't believe them, though, and a lot of people lost their lives. She kept running, but held on to copies of the documents.

"When your mother took the job, she had no clue who she was working for, she just knew she was pregnant and needed the money to take care of you, Avery. It looked like a great job with flexible hours. Somewhere, while on the run, she met your dad and they both fell off the map. Campone didn't find them, but he never stopped looking. He knew your mother kept the final ledger she was working on, but he suspected she made copies of her other work as well. If she had involved the police, your mother had the power to take down his entire empire with one blow. The night she died, something spooked her and she took the documents with her, trying to move them to a safer place. The bulk of her documents burned in the fire, but several are missing."

"How do you know?" I ask.

Sean answers, "Based on the recovered pieces, it appears that several pertinent documents were not in the stack. She put what she was carrying in the glove box, so the center of the stack wasn't consumed by the fire. The most damning ledgers she worked on are still out there somewhere."

That's why my mother was always so on edge. That's why she was compulsively cleaning that spot in the cabinets. She probably did it without noticing. When I was younger, she'd tell Daddy to pack up, and we'd take off for an awesome vacation in a blink. I thought it was her being fun, but this makes me see her in a whole new light. Mom was scared. She was afraid of them finding her right up until the night she died. If I'd not found the coffee can, I wouldn't believe any of this, but I did find it. I know she was frightened.

My throat feels unbearably dry, and my body begins to tremble. I tense, trying to stop it, not wanting to share this heartache with them. It's a piece of me they'll never know, tand I want to keep it that way.

"What's in these documents that's worth killing for?"

Sean's lip twitches and one side pulls up into a crooked smile. "What you'd expect—secrets, money, power. Every illegal transaction between Campone and half of New York's elite: businessmen, congressmen, old money, and new money. Victor didn't discriminate; he accepted anyone's money freely. *Everything* in those documents is damning. Your mother worked as a bookkeeper at a small grocery store in Ronkonkoma. She was a smart woman, but she didn't realize who was on the other end when she started tugging on that thread. Her world unraveled. She ran, hid, and took what she found with her. My guess is that she kept the documents hidden to use as leverage if Campone ever captured her or a member of her family. The night she died, those documents were being moved to a vault. Campone's men took the opportunity to tie up loose ends and slammed a drunk driver into their car."

"How?" I blink back tears and swallow hard. "How could you know all this, all this time, and not tell me?"

Sean stands there, rigid, unblinking. "Some things are better left alone. This is one of them. You had no idea what was happening, but you're being played move by move, inching toward an early grave."

"And I suppose your name is in those papers?"

Sean shakes his head. He opens his mouth to speak and then steps away, turning his back on me.

"Answer me! This isn't a game, Sean! I thought you died! I thought Marty killed you!"

When he turns back to look at me, Sean's voice is cold. "It doesn't matter."

"The hell it doesn't! You knew I love you, and you used that against me! But why am I surprised? I should have seen this coming. Falling in love with a Ferro is dangerous. They steal your heart and destroy your soul. Well, you know what? I'm not dead yet."

We stare at each other for way too long. Sean works his jaw, not wanting to answer, but I already know he's going to deny ever feeling anything for me. The thing is I know it's a lie—I feel it. The tension between us is hot and palpable. Marty senses it too, based on the way he stands at the window, giving us more space. One man admits he cares about me, the other won't. I roll my eyes and stand up. I think I'm going to be fine, but everything spins and I fall into Sean's chest.

He catches me quickly in those strong arms and holds me to his chest. Looking into his face, I try one last time. "Why won't you say it? Sean, I know how you feel."

"I tried to return you."

"The key word there is *tried*. You *tried* to return me, but then you bought me again and again after that."

Sean watches me and tries not to smile. His voice drops to a whisper, "I tried to love you, the way you want, the way you need and it nearly got you killed." He tangles his fingers in my hair and lifts my chin. "This needs to end, *we* need to end if you want to walk away alive."

Silence spans between us, becoming deafeningly loud.

Sean finally breaks the silence, "I want the documents."

"I don't have them." Defiant, I lie to his face.

"I know you do. There's been a squatter in a home I recently acquired. You wouldn't happen to know her, would you?" Sean looks so smug. I shove him away, and he has the audacity to smile at me.

"You bought my parents' house?"

"Campone bought it before me, trying to find the documents. His men searched every inch of that home and came up with nothing, but I saw you climbing around the kitchen. Want to tell me what you found?"

"Mom's cash stash. No papers."

"Don't do this, Avery." Sean's brow bunches together and his voice is strained. "I can't protect you from this."

"Obviously." Glancing at Marty, I add, "and neither can he. You two brought the damn mafia in tow." Sean and I are standing, facing each other, gazes locked. "Since it seems I have a limited life expectancy, I want to leave. Now."

Sean blocks me after I twist out of his grip. "No, not until you tell me where they are."

"Campone is dead, Sean."

Sean gets in my face, and his warm breath washes over my lips as he rants. "His men aren't, Avery. There's a power vacuum and every single one of those guys is trying to find you, torture you, and make you wish you were dead. We can help you. Give me the documents, and Marty will get you out of here."

"Why not you?" As soon as I ask the question, Sean's gaze drops, almost as if he's ashamed, and I know his plan. He's trying to take Campone's place. I knew Sean had some shady business dealings, but this isn't like him. It can't be true. But the way he moves away from me says volumes.

"Marty, take her back." Sean steps away from me and walks out of the room.

Marty puts his hand on my arm to lead me out of the house, but I shake it off, storming after Sean instead. "Come back here! You can't do this! Have you lost your mind? You're a businessman, not a crime lord. Sean Ferro, stop!"

I follow Sean out of the room, up some stairs and into an upstairs hallway, yelling at him all the way, though he doesn't appear to hear me. Marty doesn't follow.

Chapter 7

Sean storms into a little room, and I burst in behind him. It's not until we're inside that he rounds on me. Moving swiftly, both his hands are suddenly coming at my head. He uses his body to slam me back into the door as it shuts behind me.

Sean's fists are on either side of my head, his nose touching mine, he breathes in my face, "You have no idea who I am or of what I am capable. I admit, I'm infatuated with you and always have been. But you are a diversion, and right now that's a very bad thing for both of us."

My heart thumps rapidly in my chest, my body screaming for me to run, but I can't move. Sean is pressing into me, crushing me, holding me in place. "This isn't you," I say softly.

"That's where you're wrong, because this is me. I am a monster and always have been. It's not part of me, *it is me*. Whatever you think you saw wasn't real. I used you like you used me."

"I did not use—"

"You did," he breathes in my face, pressing in nearer. "Every hour of every day has been about getting what you want. Well, what you want and what I want don't match. They never have. I said what you wanted to hear to get what I need and I need those documents. I want them, Avery, and I will do anything I have to do to get them. Make no mistake about that." Sean pushes off the wall and suddenly he's across the room, looking out the window at the ocean.

I catch my breath and watch him, staring in silence. This is the end of my old life, I can feel it. What I was yesterday is gone—that girl no longer exists. Sucking in the cool night air, I move across the room and step up behind him. Hesitantly, I reach up, hand shaking, but stop without touching him.

Bringing my hand back to my side, I say, "I know you feel guilty about Bryan, about what happened, but it doesn't have to go this way. Even if you don't want to be with me, you don't have to do this."

"It's not about you. It never was. You're a nuisance, a mite that crawled under my skin and distracted me from my goals."

His words make me want to cry, but I blink them back. I know what he's doing; he's trying to push me away. He lied to me, drugged me, and faked his shooting. It's the aftermath of Bryan's death that has him like this. He's not spoken of it, but I can sense it. He blames himself. If things with Bryan hadn't gone down the way they did, I'd have Sean talking about white picket fences.

"Fine," I manage without a tremor in my voice. "How do I get you the documents?"

He rounds on me. "You have them?"

I nod. "I think so. If I'm right, I'll give them to you under one condition."

"You're in no position to be stipulating conditions, Miss Smith." The corners of his mouth twitch at the use of my pet name.

"Oh I think I am, Mr. Jones. You see I have something you want."

"That something that will get you killed if you keep it."

"Yes, but you won't kill me to get it." I pat my palms together and look up at him.

Sean smirks, making my pulse race faster. A wolfish smile crosses his lips. "Why on earth would you think that?" He moves toward me, one pace at a time, his body language more menacing than ever. "After everything I've done, why do you still think you can save me?

Some people are just destined for Hell. You can't stop it."

"You're not there, yet."

Sean smiles down at me, taking a piece of hair and tucking it behind my ear. "I could have pushed you too far so many times. I could have broken you like I broke that girl, like I broke my wife. That's what you fail to see, Avery. I don't have demons, I am a demon. Every second I'm in your life will cause you more and more pain. Agony will have a new meaning after this, so don't play games with me. You can't win."

The stupidest idea I've ever had crosses my mind. The information in those documents could be used to own every powerful family on Long Island, including the Ferro family. Eyes locked, my lips twist into a grin. "You're all bark, Sean. You always have been, and this whole time we've been together, I've learned your tricks, your moves. Maybe I didn't see them before, but it's clear now." I pace around him as I talk, and sound more confident than I feel. "The way I see it, as long as the documents are in my possession, I own you. If I take Miss Black's job, I'll own everyone. I won't need you to protect me, because Black won't want to lose me, and if those papers happen to end up in the hands of a reporter, well, I'm guessing the Ferro family would be ruined." I stop in front of him, and look up into his face.

Anger and pride are warring within him. He enjoys it when I act this way, but he fears it, too. It means I understand him more, that I'm not the innocent girl he first met. It means I'm more like him. As I speak, his blue gaze narrows, his hands ball into fists, and he folds his arms over his chest. He laughs in my face. "You think you can take Campone's place?"

"I know I can."

Chapter 8

There have been a handful of times I've truly been afraid around Sean, where my gut tells me to flee or fight. This is one of them. My words have broken something inside his brain and, I swear to God, I heard it snap. His blue eyes narrow and he looks ready to break free, ready to allow the animal trapped within to escape. Using his body like a bulldozer, he pushes me back into the wall, his normal emotionless expression regaining control of his face.

In a lethal voice, he lowers his head so we're nose to nose. "Don't you dare!"

"You can't stop me." Heart pounding, I hold my breath, ready to scream. The vein on the left side of Sean's head looks like it's going to pop it's throbbing so fast. "You said yourself, whoever gets those documents wins. I have them. I win."

"I have you, so you lose."

"Mel will kill you if you hurt me."

Sean laughs and backs away. The sound frightens me, because it's so far removed from what he normally sounds like. It's not a sound of joy, it's a chime of something dark. "Don't you get it? Everyone around you was a plant: cops, narcs, even assholes like me. Everyone around you wants to be first to get to your mom's stashed documents. She made a fatal error, taking the documents with her. I'm sure she thought they'd be leverage, but in the end they just led to her early demise, and they will do the same to you. You can't keep them. It's not an option."

"What are you saying?"

"Mel is playing you just like everyone else. There's no one you can trust, Avery. There's nowhere to go."

Trystan's name pops into my head. There's no way he's involved in all this. It's as if Sean knows what I'm thinking and laughs that horrible sound again. "He can't protect you, but I'm sure he'd give you what you want. A little house and a baby are right up Scott's alley. He'll get the family he never had. Go back to him. You're perfect for each other. Just give me the documents first."

His reaction to Trystan throws me off. My face scrunches together as I try to decipher his meaning. "*Go back to him? You think I belong with Trystan? Is that why you've gone nuts?*"

"You were already with him." My body stiffens without meaning to and a chill runs over my skin. Sean glances at me out of the corner of his eye. "It's fine."

"No, it's not fine. I don't even know what happened that night, so how can you be so sure?" The memory of Trystan's kisses lights up in my mind. I wanted him so badly, but I really just wanted him to be Sean. "Things didn't progress very far."

"Scott told me he'd steal you if I didn't treat you better. Imagine, all it took was Mr. Big Shot dropping his pants and you fell at his knees like a cheap whore. Wait a second..." Sean smiles at me, as if he couldn't care less.

My shoulders square off. "You told him to take care of me. He did."

"I didn't tell him to nail you."

"He didn't."

"You two looked pretty cozy together." The anger fades from his face. Sean runs his hand through his hair. "It doesn't matter anymore. Just give me the documents and go back to Scott. It'll ensure your survival and his."

"Sean, I wanted you, you dumbass!" I'm so livid, so furious, and so afraid he's going to walk out that door, ruining his life and mine. "I've always wanted you!"

The corner of his lip twitches up and then falls. He steps toward me. Gazing down into my face he breathes, "I want things that would make your skin crawl.

What I want is so far past what you want, what you need, that you can't even fathom it. The things I'd do to you," he bites his lower lip and lowers his gaze to my chest and back to my eyes, "you'd never forgive me. That's what I want. That's what I need. We're incompatible, so it's time to stop pretending. You go on with your life and play the happy wife, while I do what I have to do."

"Sean, it doesn't have to be like this."

"It does." His jaw locks, as if he's keeping himself from saying more. Sean walks out the door without another word.

Chapter 9

Peter stands next to his car, scanning the dunes for me. I have no idea what to tell him. Sean's lost his mind. When Peter sees me, he runs over. "Are you hurt?"

I shake my head and tell him what Marty told me to say. "Sean's fine. Marty took him because it was an easy way to get to me." The lie tastes like acid in my mouth, burning my tongue as I speak it. Peter is a great guy and I don't want him hurt because of me. Sean and Marty made sure that Sean's brothers would be safe. Their plan provides safety for everyone if Sean is able to take over Campone's criminal activities. Peter can't know, and I won't tell him. He's been kind to me, and I don't want him to get hurt.

"Where did he take you?" Peter opens the car door for me, waits for me to get in, then he shuts it gently behind me, ever the gentleman.

"I don't know. He just wanted to talk to me."

"About what?" Peter jumps into his seat and we shoot across the bridge like it's on fire. He can't get me away from here fast enough. I feel like I'm going to puke. This is the part where I have to decide who to trust and who to cut free. I trust Peter, but I like Sidney. I want to make sure Peter makes it to their wedding.

I stare at the water racing by my window, repeating the things I was told to say. Sean will be deposited at the Babylon train station at midnight and Marty will flee. But that's not what will really happen. Instead, Marty will turn himself in and Sean will drop the charges. Marty will pay a few fines and everything will be like it was before, except now I know the truth. Up until now, I thought the person I needed to be afraid of was Miss Black. Now, she seems to be the least of my worries.

Peter's voice reaches through my thoughts. "Avery?"

"Hmm?" I glance over at him. I'd been staring at the causeway, and mentally drifted from the conversation.

"So, no ransom?"

I shake my head. "No, it was personal. With Marty, it's always been personal. He loves me." He told me to say that. It's the only excuse for his behavior that everyone will swallow without question. "He tried to get me to forgive him. I said I couldn't, that I love Sean." My voice cracks, because after all this time, after all these tales, I finally get to tell someone the truth. But it won't matter because once Sean does this, there's no going back.

I was full of it when I said I could take Campone's place. I'd be dead in a day. That man was a lunatic, killing as he pleased. The part of Sean that feeds on fear and control will thrive in that life. I can't let it happen, but I don't know what to do. Glancing at Peter, I watch the side of his face, wondering if I should tell him everything. The Ferro family is full of devious people, but Peter isn't a Ferro, not anymore.

I could go to Constance for help, but it's possible she's already one of the players in this game. Mel is a question mark, so is Gabe. Amber and Naked Guy are dead because of this, because of me. Bryan is dead too, and Sean is throwing away his cousin's gift by doing this.

I can't allow it. I won't let him do this. Somewhere inside Sean is a man that's protective and will sacrifice himself to save everyone else. He did it to save the memory of Amanda and now he's doing it to save me. I need help. By the time I decide to say something to Peter, we're passing Babylon Village and getting farther east. I didn't even ask where we're going. I just got into his car and let him drive.

"Peter, I need to ask you something."

"Shoot."

Once I say these words I can't take them back. Peter has a life ahead of him. Peter escaped this life and all the crap that comes with it. But without him, Sean will die. He'll fall deeper into Hell and become the demon he thinks he is. "Peter, I—"

Before I can tell him, his phone rings. SEAN FERRO lights up on the screen. "Oh, thank God." Peter clicks the green button and answers on speaker. "You had us worried, bro. Avery said he didn't want you. You ok?"

"I'm fine." Sean sounds pissy, but doesn't come across with the strength I know he has—he's going to blindside them all. Every one of Campone's men will think Sean is weak, recovering from a bullet wound. They won't see what hit them until it's too late. Sean is planning a lot more than he said, that much I'm sure. "That little shit was just trying to scare me. I'm in Babylon, at the train station. Any chance you could head this way."

"No problem, we were just passing through. I'll be there in ten." The line goes dead. Peter lets out a sigh of relief. "I couldn't stand to lose him, too. Not after everything we've been through. He doesn't talk about it much, but Amanda's death hit him really hard, and the trial nearly destroyed him. Sean wants to be a pillar of steel, but he's not. No one can hold it together that long and not break. If I didn't have Sidney," he shakes his head and lets out a nervous laugh. Glancing at me, he tips his head. "What were you saying?"

Peter turns onto Montauk Highway, heading toward the station. My gut squeezes hard. He's going to lose Sean. There's no way to get out of this and keep Peter's family intact. I stare at the dashboard, thinking.

"Avery?"

"I can't tell you." I look over at him, wishing that I could.

"Are you in trouble?" Peter's worry lines crease deeper as he glances from me to the road. He slows his approach to the station. "Talk to me. Maybe I can help."

"I know you can help, but it's bad, Peter." Staring at my hands I try to figure out a way to get his advice without involving him, but flounder. "I'm in some messed up stuff, up to my neck."

"We've all been there. Talk to me, I can help."

"You haven't been here, Peter. I can promise you that. I don't think anyone in your family has, and I want to keep it that way." I look up at him and our eyes meet. He catches my meaning.

"Sean is trying to save you, isn't he?" I nod. "But he won't be able to save himself."

"That." The word sticks in my throat. "What do I do?"

"Tell me everything so I can help you." Peter pulls the car over and stops. We're still in town, not far from my parent's old house. "Avery, that's one thing Sean has never understood—he doesn't have to do everything alone."

"He won't ask you for help, and I can't steal your life. That's what will happen if you help me. I'm going to get out and walk away. Take care of Sidney." I push the door open and hop out onto the sidewalk.

"Avery, get back in here. Mel said to bring you back. I can't let you walk around alone."

"You need to save your brother. Don't worry about me. Please, just believe me. I'll do what I have to do. You keep Sean in your sight and don't leave his side. He can't do what he's planning if you're there. He won't take you down with him. Promise me you'll watch out for him."

"Avery, I will, but—" Peter is about to say more, but I shut the door. Turning on my heel, I hurry down the street, losing myself in the crowd. I hear his voice calling me back, but I can't do it. I need to get to the house before Sean, before he has a chance to save me and destroy himself.

Chapter 10

I go in the house through the back
door and run into the kitchen, grabbing
the coffee can. I remove most of its
contents, leaving the envelopes and
some of the other things inside. My
cheap jacket has an inside pocket; I stuff
the money and the papers inside it and
zip them shut, clutch the coffee can
under my arm and head for the back
door.

As I pull it shut, Sean's voice comes from behind me. "Hand it over, and walk away."

Turning slowly, I hate myself for what I'm about to do, but I have to— there's no other way. Shaking my head, I hold onto the can tighter. "Don't do this, please. There has to be another way. Sean, you don't have to pretend. You don't have to martyr yourself to save me."

He stares at me, those blue orbs unblinking. "This isn't for you. It's not even about you." He steps closer, closing the space between us. "It's about me and always has been. Get that through your head."

"You're a bad liar, especially when it comes to protecting someone you love."

"I don't love you."

"You mean you don't want to love me, but you do. You mean you can't stand the thought of losing me, so you're doing this. You've ensured that everyone is safe, everyone except you. This will destroy you, Sean. You can't do this." I tighten my grip on the coffee can and move it farther from him.

Sean reaches out and rips it from my hands. "Too bad, because I just did." He opens the lid, sees the envelopes, and then seals the can again. "Stay out of sight for a few days."

"I won't let you do this."

"You already have." He smiles at me and shakes the can, before turning on his heel. Sean's shoulders are squared and rigid. He doesn't look back.

Chapter 11

Before Sean even gets to his car, I start fence hopping. Soon, I'm half a mile away with too many houses and streets between us to count. I run and catch a bus that's just pulling away from the curb. The driver stops and lets me on. "Thanks," I say.

The driver nods as I pay and head toward the back, out of sight. The driver closes the doors and moves on, winding up and down the streets until we're on the highway. It's not the best place to read, but it might be the only chance I have. I pull out a document and start reading, but it doesn't make sense. I pull out another and another, scanning, reading as fast as I can. The bus rolls along, and I doubt Sean is far behind me.

The next time the bus stops, I look up and an old woman takes the seat next to me. She glances at my papers and chuckles to herself. "I haven't seen that kind of shorthand in a long time."

"Shorthand?"

She nods. "It was commonly used about fifty years ago. I used it when I was a secretary in my early twenties, but then I married the boss." She nudges me with her shoulder and laughs.

"So you can read this?"

She nods. "Of course."

"Can you show me how?"

"Sure, it's not hard once you understand it." She takes a page and smiles. "The woman who wrote this was Italian, or at least she knew enough that it poked out now and again. Like this word, it's not English, so that probably makes it harder for you to translate. Do you know where these documents are from?"

I shake my head. "They were my mother's. She died and I found them while going through her things."

"I'm sorry for your loss, dear." Her old eyes scan the papers with renewed interest. She begins to laugh, shaking her head. "Well, your mother was a pip. She interchanged things. See this word? Iron? It's a name, not a piece of metal. This mark here means it's an account, see?"

Shaking my head, I look at the papers. "No, I'm sorry, I don't get it."

She points, "This column lists names, and this one has notes about them. See, Iron means Ferro—oh, that's odd. Did she know the Ferro family? This mark here means that a sum of money was received and added to this account. Here's the total. She's made a notation that those funds weren't found when closing the store—she must have been a bookkeeper. She matched the slip tape with the customer number. Smart woman. It's just an account record, dear. Boring reading materials for a pretty little thing like you to be reading on the bus." She smiles again, and pushes up. "Well, this is my stop. I've got to go to CVS before heading home. Have a good night."

I watch her walk down the aisle toward the exit, wondering if she's a threat. I stay on the bus for the next few stops and am able to make out some of the names, including more entries for Ferro, the iron family. I wonder if Constance did this, or if it was Sean's father.

Stuffing the papers back in my jacket, I jump off at the next stop. I've traveled east for a comfortable distance from my parents' house and it's getting late. Exhaustion starts to cloud my brain. Near the bus stop, I find a rundown motel. I walk up to the front desk, pay cash for the next few days, and before long, I'm in an old room that smells as bad as it looks. The walls are covered in wood paneling and there's an old orange carpet on the floor. This place has hourly rates and it sounds like a couple is making use of that feature in the room next door. Stomping from the room above causes plaster from the dated popcorn ceiling to fall on my head, but I'm too tired to care. The second I hit the bed, I pass out.

Chapter 12

SEAN

Wooden boards, blistering and sun-bleached, are warm under my feet. The ocean laps quietly at the small dock, making it sway slightly, as I take one step and then another. A lighthouse flashes in the distance, spinning its narrow beam of light, momentarily blinding me. I take another step. There are very few left before I fall. Time is failing me, and the inky waves will swallow me whole.

Pulse pounding, I take another step, placing my bare foot on the splintering wood, cursing my inability to go back where I was, back to that place with her. I felt safe there and thought I could be someone else. For her I changed, and for her, I'll die.

I step forward, inching toward my demise. My throat tightens in fear, but my feet won't stop. My end is inevitable. I won't turn back and I have no other way out.

"Sean!" His voice startles me at first, but when I hear him again, clearly calling my name, I shield my eyes and peer through the darkness. I see nothing for miles, no land, and no place to rest. "Sean," he says again, "step out."

I hear his voice, but I can't see his face. "You shouldn't be here."

"Neither should you. I did what I had to do; now you need to trust me. Have faith, Sean. Step out. The waves will carry you to the other side."

A flicker of light catches my eye and a familiar voice comes from behind me. I turn, looking back at the lingering rays.

"Come back to me, Sean." Amanda's words cut through me, and I fall to my knees on the dock. "Come home." She repeats the last words she ever said to me, over and over again, beckoning me back.

Their voices clash like clanging cymbals, each pulling me in a different direction. The mistakes of my past call me back to my wife, while my cousin calls me forward. I failed him. Avery knows. She figured me out.

She belongs with Trystan.

"Come home."

I cringe and lean forward, resting my head on the dock. Everything within my body is screaming out for me to turn back, to return to Amanda. I did this to her. I caused her death.

"Sean, step out. Keep going! Don't stop!" Bryan calls to me again in that tone he used so often. I can't bear what happened the night we went to get Hallie. Everything went wrong and before I knew what happened, he was gone.

The certainty of Amanda's light beckons to me, calling me back, but Bryan's voice is strong, pulling me forward. "It was my choice, Sean, not yours. It was my choice, not yours. Don't waste this chance. Step into the water and you'll be safe."

It takes every ounce of strength within me to pull my leaden body up off the dock and haul my feet forward. Every moment is agony, every second is torture, but I finally step off the end. Amanda's voice falls silent and the only sound remaining is the ocean. When my foot hits the water it sinks. I turn to look back at the dock, but it's gone. Amanda's light has disappeared. There's no way back and no way forward. I'm sinking. The cold water is swallowing me whole.

I picture the liquid noose rising around my neck, cold and strong. I picture the waves pulling me under as if they were the arms of a giant. I picture gasping for air but never finding enough.

Suddenly my feet hit rock, as if I were standing in a shallow puddle. It's an illusion, the way the darkness plays off the top of the water makes it look like an ocean, but it isn't. I take off at full-speed, running toward the lighthouse, wanting her, knowing she's there. Avery is my rock in the storm. That's what Bryan was telling me.

Elated, I push further ahead, faster. When I make it to the lighthouse, I race up the steps to the room at the top and throw open the door. The woman I love turns to look at me, and my heart tears in two. She's naked, standing wrapped in the arms of Trystan Scott. I try to say her name, but my voice fails me. I move my mouth, but she regards me as no more than a speck of dust. The light turns toward me once more, blinding me.

I shield my eyes, calling out to her. "Avery! Wait! I lied. I want you; I want a life with you. Please, Avery…"

But it's too late. When the light spins around again she's gone.

Chapter 13

SEAN

Drenched in cold sweat, I dart upright in my bed, gasping air as fast as I can swallow it.

"Avery." I say her name without thinking, and a chill goes up my spine. Clutching my head in my hands, I throw my feet off the side of the bed and sit for a moment, willing my pulse to resume a normal rate. My stomach twists in knots, twisting increasingly harder and tighter, even though the nightmare is over. But that's the problem—the nightmare is not over, it never ends.

"God, I hate this place." I can't believe I let Pete talk me into coming here. The house I grew up in conjures more nightmares than anywhere I've ever slept, but Peter insisted on it. There's no getting it out of his head that I'm injured, and since I need them to believe I am, I allow him to take me here.

If I see my mother, I'll lose it. I know I will. Our last discussion was less than amiable. Just one disagreement with her would be a fucking cakewalk, but that woman is ruthless. Her scheming never ends and it wouldn't shock me in the least to see her name at the top of Avery's damned papers.

A promise is a promise, blood be damned. I did this, but Avery doesn't know why. I intend on keeping it that way. Lies suit me. I've told so many lies the truth is irrelevant at this point. There's no way she can possibly navigate her way between fact and fiction. For that, I feel sick. She didn't deserve this, not any of it, and she wouldn't be in this goddamn mess, were it not for me.

There's only one way for her to get out. I'm in this so deep the only direction to go is down, further into decay. I know I'll lose what's left of myself; I'm not a fool. Avery's nothing if not perceptive, but there are no choices left. I won't abandon her.

Laughing to myself, I shake my head and push my sweaty hair out of my face. If I had never gone to Mother for help, this wouldn't have happened. That snake has her fangs at my neck, ready to strike, and Avery is positioned to fall in my wake. My one desperate action caused this path of destruction.

Cracking my knuckles, I stretch and look up at the ceiling. My days are numbered. My time is devolving into seconds and although I'm horrified by the thought of what I have to do, no dream can make me change course. I have to see this through, or die trying.

Pushing off the bed, I pad across the floor and grab the coffee can off my dresser. Peeling back the lid, I peer inside and smirk. I was livid last night when I finally opened the envelopes. I can't believe she tricked me—no, that's not true—I can believe it. She's been trying to save me since we met. For every move I made, she had an equally brilliant countermove. She stole my breath the first time I saw her, and owned my soul from the first time I kissed her. She's my equal, my counterpart in every way. The darkness that stains her soul is as black as mine. Malice is under those stains, waiting to be raised to the light.

If Avery can convince Mother or Black to support her, she'll beat me to the draw, and secure her place at the head of Campone's organization. That power struggle will fizzle and die; no one in their right mind would challenge Avery with those benefactors. Mother and Black are two of the scariest women of all time. When I read the bible story about the Garden of Eden and the snake is first mentioned, these ladies come to mind. Both have loved me, yet neither would hesitate to spill my blood if doing so meant getting something they want.

I look down at the empty envelopes and then dump the trinkets into my hand one more time, wondering why Avery let these treasures escape. I think of her cross necklace, how she lost it and how long it took me to find it again. It pains me that she tossed these away.

She's changing, and not for the better. I have to stop her.

Avery thinks she can prevent me from taking this path, but she's just made me more determined. I know she still has the documents and I plan to take them back. Until then, just the illusion that I have them in my possession will turn all the attention toward me. I know they saw me rip the can from her hands last night.

The only loose end is Avery, if someone tries to hurt her, they'll hurt me. She's a piece of me, as important as my hand and more precious than my soul.

If she's with Scott, they can't get near her—not with his security entourage. The thought sickens me, but it's where she belongs. I can't give her what she wants— the pretty little house, the white picket fence, and the baby—he can.

"You chose this shit, Ferro." I mutter to myself and walk across my old room to look out the window. It's morning. The sunrise looks like spilled paint cutting across the darkness.

She's out there somewhere, waiting. I need to find her before they do.

Clutching the windowsill, and leaning toward the glass, I say to myself, "This ends today." I'll do what I have to—how could I do anything else? I'll defend my family, even if I die doing it. Pete doesn't deserve this shit; he deserves a good, long and happy life with Sidney, away from all this drama. As for Jon, God knows he's just clueless. He's barely been on his own and is so wrapped up in some girl he can't think straight. Now that Bryan is dead and took the blame for me, Jon is too distraught to be of any help.

Not that any of them could help me right now, anyway.

I'm on my own.

Chapter 14

~AVERY~

A knock on the motel room door wakes me from dreamless sleep. I roll over, ignoring it, but just as I close my eyes, the soft knocking comes again.

Tap. Tap. Tap.

My heart jumps and I sit up slowly, and wait, panic flooding through me. I slip out of bed, still in my clothes, and pad silently to the door. I've just leaned forward to look through the peephole, when the knob begins to rattle. I jump back, terrified. Glancing around, I try to find a weapon, but there isn't anything that's not glued down. I grab the only thing that I've got—a pencil.

There's a click and the door swings open. Rain is barreling down in buckets, pouring over the man standing in my doorway. It's too dark to make out his face. He steps into the room and looks up.

"Sean."

He's breathing hard, his clothes soaked and clinging to his skin, highlighting each well-defined muscle. "I need those papers. Do you have any idea what you've done? You nearly got me killed." His anger surges as he slams the door and rushes toward me.

I yelp and stumble backward, falling onto the bed. The springs squeak beneath my weight, as I try to crabwalk away, but Sean grabs my ankles and pulls me forward. He leans down and gets in my face. "I'm going to ask you one more time, Miss Smith. Where are your mother's documents?"

"I don't have them." Heart beating hard, I stay still beneath him. Sean's hands work their way up my legs, patting, feeling for the paper, but it's not there. He manhandles my body, searching, but there aren't any papers stuffed into my clothes.

"Avery," he huffs in my face and presses me back into the bed, crawling on top of me as he does so, "so help me, God, you've pushed me too far." Maybe my fear brought this out in him, or maybe it was his own anger, either way, as he leans into me I can feel how much he wants me. Water beads off his hair and drips onto my neck. His eyes follow the drops as they slide across my curves and disappear between my breasts.

"Same here." My voice trembles, and I try to push him away, but he presses me further into the bed with his body.

Our lips are so close that I can feel his breath, and the way he's pressing into me makes me shiver. It's as if he knows what I'm thinking, how much I want to be with him, how much I wish we could just start over and put everything behind us.

Sean glares at me with those steely eyes. "We can't."

Brushing my lips against his, I whisper, "But you want to."

"You can't do what I need right now, what I want." Sean is about to pull away, when I reach for him, taking hold of the back of his neck.

"Try me."

Two words. That's all it takes to break him. Sean darts upright and pulls off his wet jacket and shirt, leaving only his jeans. He kicks off his boots and climbs urgently back on top of me. His eyes are hungry, devouring me like a starving man. He doesn't speak. His head dips for my neck as he presses my body to his. His lips trail over my soft skin, teasing me, leaving me gasping for breath. His hand is on the back of my neck, tangling in my hair as he yanks me up onto his lap.

With a tug, he rips off my cheap shirt and tosses it to the floor. My bra is given the same treatment. Unchecked, his strength sends a chill over my skin. The way he holds me, as if he'll never see me again makes my pulse race and takes my breath away. I want to feel my body against his, skin on skin, hot and slick, but Sean pulls away. The sudden rush of cold air makes me gasp. I reach for him and he quickly grabs my wrists, tying them together in front of me. He's careful not to make eye contact with me as he works. It seems like a movement he's mastered through practice. My heart pounds harder with anticipation and regret. I liked what we were doing a moment ago, but I told him he could do more.

When he's done, my wrists are bound tightly in front of me. A shiver works its way up my spine. He stands, setting me gently on the floor. Sean's cool blue gaze flicks up and peers at me from behind damp hair. That predatory grin spreads across his face. He circles around me, watching my chest rise and fall, tracing my body with his eyes before reaching down and ripping away my panties.

I cry out, startled by the speed with which he grabbed me. I look up to find Sean's eyes filled with lust and something more, something dark. My pulse races faster, as my heart beats harder. I wanted this. I asked for this.

"Turn." It's a single word command. I do as I'm told and turn to face the bed, my back to him. He pushes me down so I'm leaning over the side of the bed, hips in the air, my tethered wrists stretched out before me. He jumps over the bed, and hooks my tethered wrists to the bottom of the bed frame.

Up until now, I've been able to see him moving in the faint glow of the clock and a nightlight reflecting off the bathroom mirror. Sean disappears from my view and the room turns black. The red glow of the clock is gone and the nightlight is doused.

My eyes search the darkness, but I can't see anything. My pulse quickens as worry pinches my stomach. "Sean?" I call his name softly, turning my head when I think I hear something behind me.

The movement makes it easy for him to slip something over my head so I can't see. Something else comes over my face, passing my eyes and lands in my mouth. He yanks it tight, gagging me. A third cloth is looped over my head and settles around my neck. That's when I freak out. I can't see, I can't breathe, and if he chokes me I'm going to flip out. I buck my hips and scream, trying to free myself.

I can imagine him watching me, getting harder, as fear consumes me. The only way this would be worse is if he put a bag over my head. Sean pulls on the neck cloth tightening it. I try to lift off the bed, but can't because my hands are tied down. I scream into the gag and kick out behind me.

I hear the snap before the pain registers. He hit me with something thin and hard, across my ass. I kick out again, and the resulting whip is harder this time, stinging so much it brings tears to my eyes. Shivering, I try to roll over, but I can't. He pulls my make-shift collar and I still.

"Good girl." He coos in my ear, making me jump. That's when I feel his hand travel over my back, barely touching my skin, so that it raises goose bumps. "But I like it better when you fight me. Fight with me, Avery." He whips me again, harder this time. It stings so badly I'm sure he's cut my skin. The sensation makes me kick out, but he grabs my legs and spreads them apart, wedging himself between my thighs.

As I feel his hard length against me, I freeze in place. My back goes rigid as he moves, lining up with me, and pushes in. The gag muffles my high-pitched noise, but Sean could feel the truth in my response to him. It finally registers that this doesn't hurt because I'm already wet. What's wrong with me? I like this?

Sean breathes in my ear, "Stop thinking. Just act. Be the wild animal I know you are." He tugs my collar and I panic as the sensation tightens, making it feel like I can't breathe even though I can. There's no way for me to tell him to stop.

Just as the thought crosses my mind, Sean releases the collar and reaches around, clamping a nipple in each finger. "I told you to stop thinking." He squeezes hard, and then twists.

I scream into the gag and butt my hips into his. Sean moans and slips his hands up my sides, taking hold of my hair with one hand, and the collar with his other. He tugs and I buck. If I think, he pulls my hair so hard it makes me cry.

My stomach dips as I find a rhythm, pressing into him as he pounds me into the bed, using me as his plaything. Pushing up with my hands, I try to press harder into him. I'm feeling so much, worry and lust collide and I don't want him to stop. With every thrust he takes me higher and higher, wildly tugging my collar as he does so. I don't want him to stop. I need this, I need him.

At the last second, he pulls away, making me scream with frustration into my gag. Then I feel his hands turning me over, laying me on my back. Once again, he's on top of me. My hands are pinned over my head and I can't see. He pushes into me over and over again, riding me harder and harder. We rock against each other, climbing higher and higher until I finally shatter. When I scream into the gag, Sean's thrusting becomes frantic. He pushes my legs apart and slams into me harder and faster until he reaches his climax. When he does, he pulls out and leans over my stomach, letting his warmth flow over my skin. I gasp as I feel it slide down my sides and into my navel.

A moment later, I feel his tongue against my skin, hot and far from sated. He strokes my skin, licking up every last bit, until he settles onto my arm. Leaning his head on my breast, he speaks.

"You're right. That was what I wanted." The voice is wrong. I panic when I hear it and can't believe what Sean's done, until he removes the blindfold and I see Marty is the man lying on my arm.

Heart pounding, I scream, darting upright in bed, the nightmare losing its grip on me.

My body is a hot mess, covered in sweat from my mashed up nightmare. Gripping my face in my hands, I begin to tremble. Pulling my knees into my chest, I remember where I am, and keep telling myself it wasn't real. The strange thing was, until that point of the dream, I liked it.

I don't even want to consider what that means. A collar? I like breathing. It's not optional, so why the hell would I want Sean to put a collar on me? Frightened, I sit back against the headboard and push my damp hair out of my face. My body is covered in sweat, so I kick off the sheets. I wonder what nightmares are going through Sean's head tonight. They can't be worse than mine.

Chapter 15

Thank God for meal bars. For the past four days, I've been hiding in this crappy room pulling plaster out of my hair and eating the box of meal bars I grabbed before checking in. It was an added risk, but the old ladies' comment about CVS and picking up some items made me realize that I need to stay out of sight. When Sean realizes those envelopes are empty, he's going to come looking for me, and I can't move until I know what I'm doing.

I've barely slept, save that first night. My mind is filled with strange dreams when I do. Besides, I'm afraid of being discovered and my heart won't stop racing. Last night there was a knock on my door—it leads into the parking lot—and I thought he found me. But the person gave up quickly. He must have had the wrong door.

I feel like a squirrel hiding in a tree, waiting for the cats to walk away. The thing is, if they get desperate enough, they won't wait. I need to choose—Black or Constance. Both are utterly evil, but both would want these documents. If I hold back the Ferro accounts, Constance won't kill me. I already copied them to the cloud to cover my ass in case someone takes the originals. That's my exit plan. I just haven't figured out how to pull Sean away with me.

What if he wants this? The little voice in the back of my head whispers to me. It's not the first time this thought has crossed my mind.

I've been living by fear and going against my gut for too long. My gut says he's not doing this for him—that he doesn't want it. That's his carrot—that's what I can use to lure him away—but I don't know how.

I sit up on the bed and flip on the TV. The same story is playing over and over again. A blonde woman with perfectly applied makeup repeats the headline: "Marty Masterson turned himself in to authorities for the attempted murder of Sean Ferro. When Mr. Ferro explained that Masterson was his bodyguard, all charges were dropped. Masterson explains his weapon misfired causing a—" I turn it off. It's the same bullshit story they've been telling for three days. I can't believe people bought that bunch of crap.

But they did, because they released Marty and slapped him with a few fines. Strangely enough, he had all the proper permits for his gun. I'm guessing Sean did that after the fact.

I roll back onto the bed and stare at the watermarks on the ceiling.

Constance or Black?

I have to choose an ally. Now. I've waited too long already. Logically, I should go to Constance. I still don't know who Miss Black's boss is and with my luck, Black actually works for Constance. But every time I almost make up my mind to go with Constance, I feel this horrible premonition that going to Sean's mom will end with blood—and not mine. I wouldn't put it past her to shoot her own kid. That's the reason I'm still here, wearing three-day-old clothes. I'm too afraid to change or to shower, afraid to be caught off guard. It's too risky.

My head is telling me to go to Constance, but my gut is telling me not to go to either of them. So I'm stuck in an endless loop with no way out. If I try to do anything with those documents on my own, I'll get pushed in front of a train. I need someone powerful to stand with me, and I need to act before Sean finds me.

"I can't wait anymore." I make an aggravated sound and jump off the bed. I'm playing the 'lesser of two evils' game and I can't find a way to win! If it's Black, then I have to go to Constance, but if it's Constance, I have to go to Black.

Before I can blink something slams against the door. Startled I swallow a yelp. They found me. I can hear two male voices, maybe more. One is saying to hit it again. That door won't hold, so I bolt to the bathroom and lock the door. Pulse pounding, I look around, trying to find a way out. This place is an old craphole, but I see a place to hide. I climb onto the sink and then push up the drop ceiling tile. I stick my head up there and glance around for the cable holding the ceiling up. It's two tiles over. I lean over, and can barely reach it.

There's another bang and the sound of wood splintering. Male voices shout, "Find her!"

Fuck! My palms are a sweaty mess, but there's no time. The bathroom door is a piece of crap and I already hear their footsteps. I barely manage to pull myself up, slicing my palm open in the process. My ass is hanging through the ceiling tile over the shower stall when the door gives way. As it shatters below me, I slip the tile back in place with my foot and see nothing but blackness. The tiny space stinks, but I'm too frightened to care. I bite my lip to keep from screaming.

They've entered the bathroom. Their voices are louder. "She's not here."

"She didn't fucking fall off the face of the earth! She's not one of us and Ferro isn't with her!" The guys mutter ideas, but it just makes the man angrier. "I don't give a shit!"

Two seconds later another male voice chimes in. "You cannot do that!" It's an older voice that's near hysterical. "Who is going to pay for this damage? You can't just come in here and bust the place up."

"Call it a remodel, old man." They laugh.

The old guy doesn't. "I'm calling the police and then we'll see who's laughing." Before he finishes the last word there's a scream and a sickening thud.

"I'm laughing now, you son of a bitch." There's complete silence.

I feel sick. I've been hanging onto the wire with my eyes closed tight, my body curled into a ball. My legs are up into my chest and my sneakers are resting right on top of the ceiling tiles on the wire, but I know I have to keep my weight off that ceiling or it'll fall. I'm lucky the wire is holding me at all.

Frozen in place, my hands start to slip. I don't realize why until I see blood dripping onto the tile below—the wire is cutting my hands. My feet slip into the ceiling. I can't pull them up any more and my entire body is sliding down.

Don't scream. Don't scream. Don't scream.

Wildly, I try gripping the wire and pulling up. It slices my hand deeper and sends a shooting pain up my arm. I bite my tongue to keep from crying out. Blood flows down the wire from my palm, dripping rapidly onto the old tiles. They soak it up swiftly, but in a matter of seconds there's going to be blood in the bathtub.

After a few more loud bangs, their voices quiet in favor of Police sirens bellowing in the distance.

The same man says, "Move. Now. We have to find her before Ferro does."

They're gone. My heart thumps wildly in my chest as I hear tires screech. Relieved, I touch my head to the wire and let out the breath I was holding.

That's when Marty's voice booms from below me. "You can come down now." A ceiling tile shifts below me as if it were poked. "I know you're up there and you're hurt. The ceiling is turning red." Marty sighs when I don't answer and I hear him step into the tub.

As he reaches up to move the tile, I slip. I try to hold on, but the wire slices through my hands, and I can't. My hands just won't grip. I scream as I hit the drop ceiling and take it down with me. It falls on Marty a second before I do. I hear him hit the tub with a sound like a punch, right before I land on top of him, too.

Frantic, I push my hair out of my face, smearing blood everywhere. My body is screaming at me to run as the sirens get louder.

I take off and don't look back.

I manage to cut through lawns and side streets. The only people outside at this time of day are kids. Their parents are watching their cell phones, not them, so when they tug on their Mama and say a lady covered in blood ran by, no one believes them. Nice.

It's all adrenaline now. I don't consciously choose where I'm going, I just go.

The Ferro mansion isn't far from here.

I have to get to Constance before they find me.

Chapter 16

I can barely breathe when I press the bell. My body is screaming at me, begging for a moment's rest. I made it here on foot. I've spent the past few hours jumping fences and avoiding major roads. Leaves and dirt are stuck to my clothes, and there's dried blood on my face. My hands are still screaming with weeping wounds as I fall against the door. I can't stand anymore.

I expect the housekeeper will answer, as she has so many times before. I'll ask for Constance and tell her everything. This is the best way. I keep telling myself that as I try to keep my eyelids open. The burning on my palms forces tears in my eyes. I slide down the front door until I'm nearly on the ground.

That's when it opens. I fall inside and slam my head on the marble foyer floor. My vision goes fuzzy and I blink, trying to focus on the male face. Dark hair, blue eyes. "Peter?"

He laughs. "Nope. Wrong brother, Miss Smith."

"Sean? What are you doing here?"

"I live here." He leaves me on the floor at his feet. "The question is, what are you doing here?" His voice is cold, like he couldn't care less that I'm bleeding all over his mother's perfect marble.

"I need to talk to your mom." The words come out in a hushed whisper. The world goes blurry and I blink again. The lack of sleep and the fierce fear are catching up to me. My stomach knots and I dry heave twice before curling into a ball. A tear tries to escape from my eye, but I don't want him to see so I wipe it away, smearing warm sticky blood all over my cheek.

His stance shifts from heartless to hurt. "Shit, Avery. I wish things didn't have to be this way."

I cough as a shiver rakes through me. "You get to choose the way things are."

"If only things were so simple." He kneels down and scoops me up. "Lean into me." Sean barks out an order for someone to clean up the mess I just made. He carries me away, cradling me in his arms like a child. Effortlessly, he walks up the grand staircase and navigates the winding halls of the mansion until he opens a door. We slip inside and he drops me on a bed, then turns and locks the door. My body tenses as I see the look in his eyes.

"You shouldn't have come here."

COMING SOON:

THE ARRANGEMENT 18
THE FERRO FAMILY

COVER REVEAL

Turn the page for a free excerpt from

Secrets & Lies

A Ferro Family Serial, by H.M. Ward

Secrets & Lies, Chapter 1

Is he serious? What an assface! I stumble through the quad, accidentally bumping shoulders with someone.

"Watch it, bitch." I look up to see a pointy-nosed girl surrounded by a pack of nasty friends, all sneering at me. I have no friends here, not yet.

The truth is, my life sucks. It's sucktacularly fucked up and I refuse to cry on the first day of college, but I'm having trouble swallowing the plate of shit my wonderful boyfriend just force-fed me. Excuse me, force-texted me. The asswipe texted me. He didn't even call. The more I think about it, the more my throat tightens. Breathing is overrated.

I mumble, "Sorry," and get the hell out of there, before they hogtie my ass and toss me down a flight of stairs. Not that I've ever seen anyone hogtied, but this is Texas, right? I'm out of my element, by far.

As I hurry away, I hear my roommate's voice ring out, "That's right, Bacon! You better run!" The girls all giggle like Chelsey just said the funniest thing they've ever heard. Great. She's leader of the bitch pack. Why can't I ever attract a psycho sans backup? My luck sucks. Have I said that? Well, bad luck is my key feature and the bane of my existence.

As I haul ass across the quad, my phone chirps. *Don't look at the screen. Don't look at it!* I chant to myself, but I can't. I have to see what he said. It might be an apology. He might be breaking up with his other girlfriend and texted me by accident. Uh, wait. That'd be worse. I think.

The thing is, we've been together since we were kids. Our parents used to joke that we'd be married one day, as if it were meant to be. It even felt like fate brought us together. On the day we met, I was playing outside when a terrified bunny chased Matt the two blocks from his house to my front yard. Running blindly, Matt mowed me down, leaving me for the bunny to attack instead of him.

Okay, this bunny was the size of a small dog and had a hunger for marigolds. In an effort to save their gardens from becoming rabbit food, the sweet little old ladies in the neighborhood were actively trying to poison it. I saved that rabbit from the wrath of the grannies and my prize was Matt. He called me cool names like Rabbit Slayer. Okay, it sounded cool in grade school, and much better than the normal nicknames kids give each other. Boogerface or Rabbit Slayer? Please. Like that's even a choice.

Matt and I have been together so long, I've forgotten what it feels like to be apart. Now the unthinkable has happened and I'm two thousand miles from home, completely on my own. Matt is everything to me.

I pluck the phone from my pocket and scan the screen.

There's this other thing…

Fuck. Like it could get worse. He already broke up with me. What's worse than that?

I type back, *I doubt it.*

No, you need to know. There's someone else. I'm in love with her, Kerry.

The prickling sensation hits the back of my eyes hard and fast. As I push through the door, I turn right and search for a bathroom. I can't fake my way through this. I can't sit here and pretend that he didn't just rip my heart out. How can there be someone else? I was his and he was mine. We were a couple. I have his damned ring on my finger. We were going to give this long distance relationship thing a chance.

But Matt didn't give it a chance.

A sob escapes my throat and my vision blurs. I race down the hallway, feeling the stares of strangers following in my wake. I can't cry now. I'm trying so hard not to, but my heart won't listen. It's curling into a ball and shriveling inside my chest. Grief takes hold of me, but I'm not crying yet. I try to find a restroom, holding back the cascade of sorrow that's building behind my eyes.

Plowing through the door, I head straight for the mirrors. There are always sinks by mirrors. I slam my books down on the counter and clutch the edge of the sink. Big gasping sobs wrack my body as I bend over the sink and stare at the white basin. Just as my tears start to fall, I see something move in the mirror. I feel eyes on me and the hairs on the back of my neck stand on end. I hadn't noticed anyone—not that I could see with my eyes full of tears.

Glancing up, I look across the room and don't understand what I'm looking at. A guy is standing by the wall. He's tall and toned, with dark hair and of standard build. At least, that's what he looks like through tears. Why is he in the girl's room? My brain is broken. I stand there and gape, not realizing that he's holding his thingy in his hand and standing in front of a urinal.

A crooked smile lines his lips when he sees me staring. "I, uh, think you're turned around."

His voice doesn't reach me. My body is in the middle of a full-fledged freak out and there's a guy in the ladies room, peeing on the wall. What the hell kind of school is this? I keep blinking, but I can't wrap my brain around what I'm seeing.

I manage to squeak out, "What?"

The guy zips up and gives me that pity look—you know the one. It says thank God I'm not you, in the nicest way possible. "You're in the men's room. The women's room is down the hall."

This can't be happening. Horrified, I lunge for my books, but he steps to the counter to pick them up at the same time. We collide and his firm body smacks into mine. I stutter something incoherent, finally getting a good look at his face. Holy hotness! I never look at other guys, but once in a while someone that is supermodel perfect catches my attention. When people like that cross your path, it's impossible to look away. His beauty is blinding, and even through tears I notice his sexy smirk, mildly amused blue eyes, and perfectly smooth skin.

Add in his hard body and holy crap. I smacked into the hottest man I've ever seen, stared at his package, and made an ass out of myself. I'm still upset, but so mortified at the same time, that I no longer think and adrenaline takes over. Heart pounding, I push off his firm chest and right myself. My mouth dangles open as I try to form words, but my balance sucks and my hip bumps the books. They topple off the counter and clatter to the floor, while the rest of my stuff slides into the sink for a swim. I can't be this catastrophe. I can't face this hot guy with raccoon eyes, unable to do anything but grunt at him like a baboon.

There aren't many ways to play off a disaster of these proportions. I decide to do the only respectable thing and run like hell. Before he can say anything else, I'm out the door and down the hall. And we're talking full out run, not that little sissy girl run. I mean full out, an axe murderer is going to chop me up, run.

I hear his voice behind me, calling me to come back. Thank God I didn't put my name in my books, yet. I have enough problems without shit like this happening. Horrified, I think about how freaking weird I had to look standing there, mascara running, just staring at his thingy. I stared. What the hell is wrong with me? Who does stuff like that?

I shove through the door at the end of the hall and fly down the stairwell. I'm outside and into the parking lot before I slow down. Rasping for air, I round the side of the building and double over, struggling to breathe. I stand for a second before sliding my back down the wall and pulling my knees to my chest.

I bury my face and let the tears fall.

Buy It Today!
SECRETS & LIES

MORE FERRO FAMILY BOOKS

NICK FERRO
~THE WEDDING CONTRACT~
*****

BRYAN FERRO
~THE PROPOSITION~
*****

SEAN FERRO
~THE ARRANGEMENT~
******

PETER FERRO GRANZ
~DAMAGED~
******

JONATHAN FERRO
~STRIPPED~
******

MORE ROMANCE BY H.M. WARD

SCANDALOUS

SCANDALOUS 2

SECRETS

THE SECRET LIFE OF TRYSTAN SCOTT

DEMON KISSED

CHRISTMAS KISSES

SECOND CHANCES

And more.

To see a full book list, please visit:
www.sexyawesomebooks.com/#!/BOOKS

CAN'T WAIT FOR H.M. WARD'S NEXT STEAMY BOOK?

★★★★★

Let her know by leaving stars and telling her what you liked about
THE ARRANGEMENT 17
in a review!

COVER REVEAL:

CPSIA information can be obtained
at www.ICGtesting.com
Printed in the USA
LVHW110812080419
613259LV00008BA/23/P